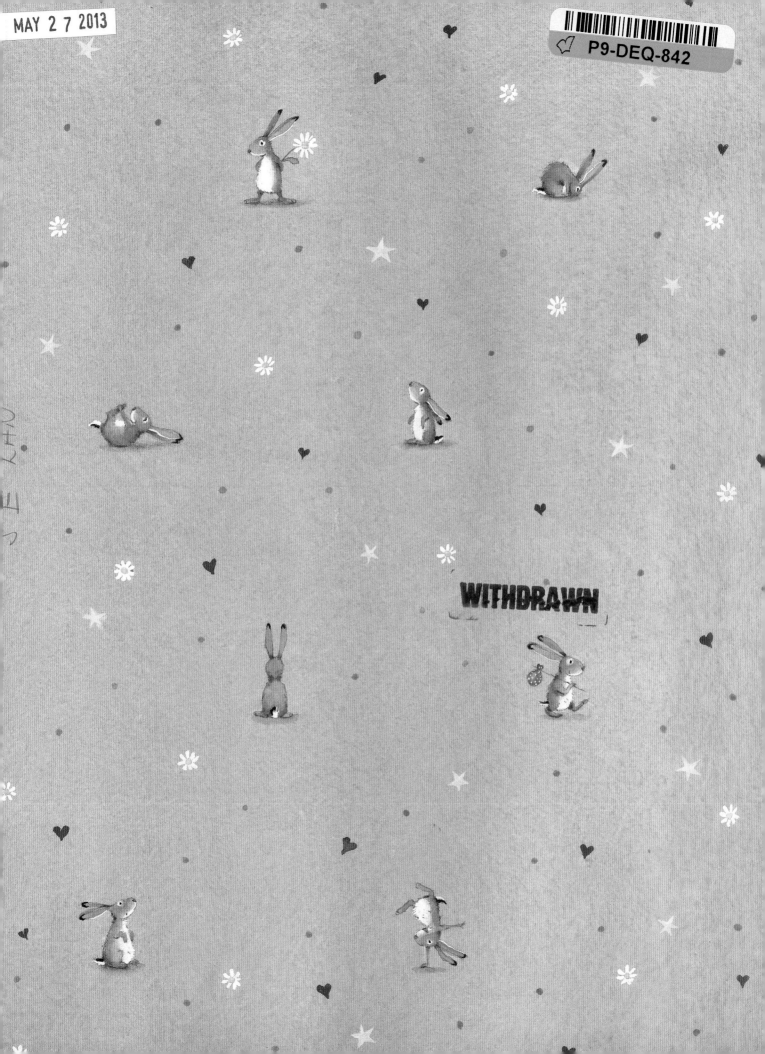

I dedicate this book to my sons, Jeremy and Jonas
—J. L.

English translation copyright © 2013 by NorthSouth Books Inc., New York 10016.
Translated by Rebecca Morrison.
Copyright © 2011 by Arena Verlag GmbH, Würzburg, Germany.
Text © 2011 by Jutta Langreuter
Illustrations © 2011 by Stefanie Dahle
First published in Germany under the title *So lieb hab ich nur dich.*

First published in the United States, Great Britain, Canada, Australia, and New Zealand in 2013
by NorthSouth Books Inc., an imprint of NordSüd Verlag AG, CH-8005 Zürich, Switzerland.
Distributed in the United States by NorthSouth Books Inc., New York 10016.

Library of Congress Cataloging-in-Publication Data is available.
Printed in China by Leo Paper Products Ltd., Heshan, Guangdong, October 2012.
ISBN: 978-0-7358-4126-0
1 3 5 7 9 · 10 8 6 4 2

www.northsouth.com

Jutta Langreuter • Stefanie Dahle

There's No One I Love Like You

North
South

Brayden Bunny was ver-r-r-y sleepy. It was late in the morning, and he still hadn't picked up his toys, washed his whiskers, or joined his sisters for their hippity-hop jumping jacks.

Mommy Bunny said, "Come along, Brayden Bunny. It's time to get up."

"I wish I could go live with my friends," mumbled Brayden.

But bunnies have very good ears, and before you knew it, Brayden's sisters' whiskers began to quiver.

Mommy Bunny heard Brayden, too, but her whiskers were perfectly still.

"You'd like to live with your friends?" Mommy Bunny asked calmly. "Which friends are those?"

"Missy Mouse, Benny Badger, Fipsi Squirrel . . . and Cousin Pepi," Brayden said, counting on his paw.

"I see," said Mommy Bunny. "And you would rather live with any one of them?"

"It . . . it'd be fun," grumbled
Brayden. "I wouldn't have to do chores."
And with that, Brayden Bunny picked up his
backpack and walked toward the door. He was very sad
to see his sisters sniffling, but now he felt as if he had to go.
"Just you wait," said Mommy Bunny. "He'll be back. You'll see."

Brayden Bunny went straight to Missy Mouse's house.

The whole Mouse family was delighted to see him. Mommy Mouse said, "I do hope you will stay with us." She ruffled his fur lovingly to make him feel welcome.

But she didn't scratch my ears like Mommy does, thought Brayden.

There was delicious root pudding for lunch,
and afterward Brayden played with Missy and her many brothers
and sisters. They drew pictures, built towers, and played dress up.

"Ouch!" yelped Brayden suddenly. "What was that?"

"Oh, you stood on a marble, that's all," said Missy.

"I almost twisted my ankle," moaned Brayden. "There's so much
stuff lying around. Don't you ever have to put your toys away?"

"Nope." Missy shrugged.

After a splendid meal of tender tulip bulbs,
they sank sleepily into bed.

During the night Brayden needed to go
to the bathroom.

It was so dark! He stumbled over the
dress-up clothes . . .

. . . knocked over the blocks . . .

. . . and on his way back, slipped on a crayon
and scared Missy's brother.

"Missy," said Brayden the following morning. "You will always
be my friend, but I cannot live here with you. There are simply too
many toys around waiting to trip up a bunny."

All the mice waved as Brayden made his way to the next family.

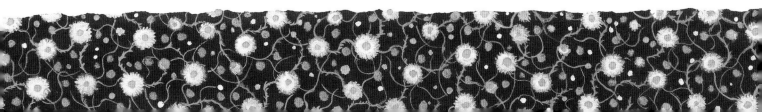

To the Badger family, that is.

"Make yourself at home, dear," said Mommy Badger. She gave Brayden a big hug.

That is very nice, thought Brayden, *but she didn't scratch my ears like Mommy does.*

There was bean casserole for lunch . . . and stuffed beetles. But Brayden didn't eat those.

There were not as many toys to fall over, and hide-and-seek was great fun in the many-caverned den.

But what was that curious smell?

Brayden shared a room with Benny and his brothers. It smelled a little funny there too. Come to think of it, Benny Badger always had a slightly unusual aroma.

The next morning, Benny said, "Breakfast is ready, then it's time to play again!"

"Don't you have to wash in the morning?" Brayden asked.

"Nope," said Benny with a laugh. "We never wash. Very occasionally we lick ourselves clean."

That explains the funny smell, thought Brayden.

"It's our famous family perfume!" Benny said.

"Benny," said Brayden. "You will always be my friend, but I cannot live here with you."

Brayden quickly washed his whiskers in the stream; then went to see Fipsi Squirrel.

The whole Squirrel family gave Brayden a merry welcome and brought him a snack of grated hazelnuts on a bed of oak leaves.

Mommy Squirrel tickled Brayden's head.

But she didn't scratch my ears like Mommy does, thought Brayden.

The Squirrels' apartment was spick-and-span—and there was no
funny smell.

Brayden spent every minute playing and giggling with Fipsi. She
showed him the many hidey-holes where her family stored their food.
Brayden would never find them by himself!

Everything would be absolutely wonderful, if only . . .

Yes, if only Brayden did not have to climb all
the way up the tree to reach the Squirrels' home!
Even with Fipsi's help, it was simply too much work!

*Our hippity-hop jumping jacks are nothing compared
to this*, thought Brayden.

He said to Fipsi, "You will always be my friend, but
I cannot live here with you."

Brayden went on his way to Cousin Pepi's.

He ran through the wide meadow and over the bridge until he saw his home.

Auntie Grace took him in her arms.

She is lovely, thought Brayden, *but she didn't scratch my ears like Mommy does*.

How wonderful it was at Cousin Pepi's. There was nothing for Brayden to trip over, no funny smell, and no house up too high—nothing was hard work.

Everything was delightful: exciting adventures with the family, fantastic games with Pepi and his friends, and fresh carrots every day. Or radishes!

I'm staying here, thought Brayden.
But there was a curious lump in his
bunny throat.

I'm staying here, thought Brayden.
But there was an odd tugging in his
bunny tummy.

I'm staying here, thought Brayden.
But there was a strange jabbing in his
bunny heart.

By the next day Brayden Bunny thought, *Everyone here
is lovely to me. I don't have to do anything I don't want to do.
I have everything I could wish for. Yet there is something—or
someone—I miss so very much.*

With a bound, Brayden seized his backpack, hurtled over the field, raced across the bridge, hopped at top bunny speed through the wide meadow, and whizzed through the woods until he reached his bunny rabbit home and burst through the front door.

"Mommy!" cried Brayden.

"Brayden!" cried Mommy. "You've come back!"

Mommy Bunny gave Brayden Bunny a big hug
and scratched his ears—as only Mommy Bunny could.
And Brayden Bunny was very happy to be home.